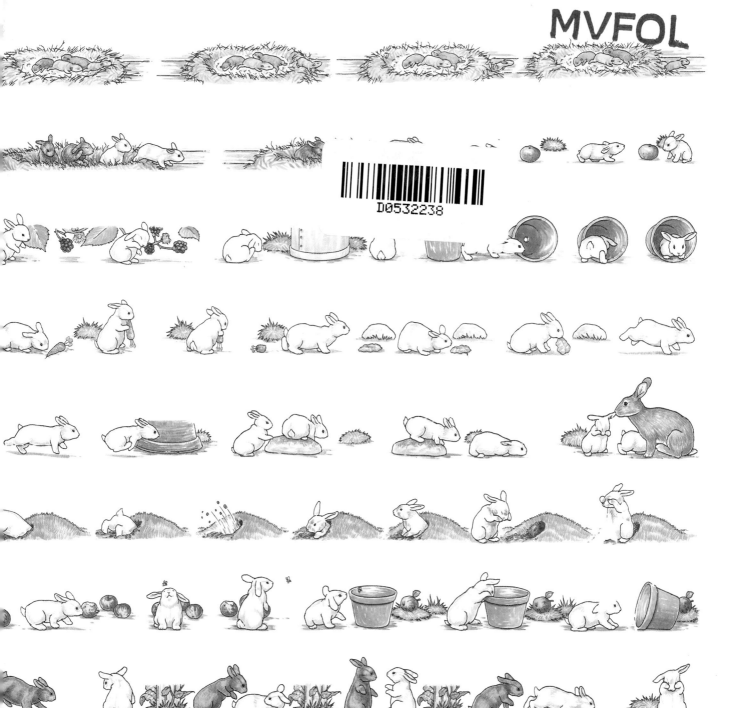

CREATED BY DORLING KINDERSLEY

Library of Congress Cataloging-in-Publication Data

Watts, Barrie.
  Rabbit/photographed by Barrie Watts.—1st American ed.
  p. cm.—(See how they grow)
  Summary: Photographs and text depict the development of a rabbit
from birth through six weeks of age.
  ISBN 0–525–67356–3
  1. Rabbits—Development—Juvenile literature.   [1. Rabbits.
2. Animals—Infancy.]   I. Title. II. Series.
QL737.L32W37 1991
599.32'2—dc20   91–97
                                                                              CIP
                                                                              AC

First published in the United States in 1992 by Lodestar Books,
an affiliate of Dutton Children's Books, a division of
Penguin Books USA Inc.
375 Hudson Street,
New York, N.Y. 10014

Originally published in Great Britain in 1991 by
Dorling Kindersley Limited, 9 Henrietta Street, London WC2E 8PS

Printed in Italy by L.E.G.O.   ISBN 0–525–67356–3
First American Edition   10 9 8 7 6 5 4 3 2 1

Written by Angela Royston
Editor Mary Ling
Art Editor Nigel Hazle
Production Marguerite Fenn
Illustrator Rowan Clifford

Color reproduction by Scantrans, Singapore

SEE HOW THEY GROW

RABBIT

photographed by
BARRIE WATTS

Lodestar Books • Dutton • New York

Newborn

I have just been born. I sleep most of the time in the nest with my brothers and sisters.

My skin is pink, and I have no fur. I cannot see or hear.

This one is me.

My mother lies on
top of us to keep
us warm.

Where is my nest?

I am one week old, and my fur is beginning to grow. It is soft and white.

Oh no! My brother and I have rolled out of the nest.

What shall we do?

Here comes my mother. She will help us back into the nest.

Looking around

I am two weeks old.
My fur is long and
thick. At last I can
see and hear.

I know the smell
of grass, and
now I can
see it too.

There are many new sounds. My sister feels afraid.

She is going back to the nest.

Out and about

I am three weeks old.
I like to leave the nest
and explore, but I do
not go very far.

Exploring makes my fur messy. I must clean myself.

I crawl along with my tummy close to the ground.

Time together

I am now four weeks old. I am
growing bigger and stronger.
My ears are growing
longer too.

My brother, sister, and I like to play near the nest where my mother can see us.

When we are tired, we snuggle close together.

Exploring

I am five weeks old.
My legs are getting
stronger.

I like playing hide
and seek in this
dark pipe.

What shall I
play next?

When I stand on
tiptoes, I am as
tall as this stone.

Getting bigger

I am six weeks old,
and now I can explore
on my own.

I can dig into the
soft earth and make
myself a burrow.

My favorite food is lettuce.
I enjoy eating the crisp
green leaves.

Next to my mother,
I am still very small.

See how I grew

Newborn

One week old

Two weeks old

Three weeks old

Four weeks old

Five weeks old

Six weeks old